W9-BTL-093

These are the Avengers

Adapted by Alexandra West

Illustrated by Derek Laufman and Dario Brizuela

Based on the Marvel comic book series The Avengers

Los Angeles
New York

MarvelHQ.com

© 2018 MARVEL

SUSTAINABLE
FORESTRY
INITIATIVE
Certified Sourcing
www.sfiprogram.org
SFI-01415

Printed in the United States of America
First Edition, April 2018 10 9 8 7 6 5 4 3 2 1
Library of Congress Control Number: 2017917458
FAC 029261-18047
ISBN 978-1-368-02353-5

These are the Avengers.

The Avengers are a
team of Super Heroes.

There are ten Avengers.
Each Avenger has a power.

Captain America is a soldier.

He has a shield.
It cannot break.

Iron Man is a genius.

Iron Man wears an iron suit.
He can fire powerful blasts.

Hulk is big.

Hulk is green.

He is strong.

Thor is a warrior.

Thor has a hammer.
He uses it to fly.

Black Widow is a spy.

Black Widow uses
her tools to fight.

Hawkeye is an archer.

Hawkeye shoots arrows.
He never misses!

Black Panther is a king.

Black Panther is fast.

He has sharp claws.

Falcon is a S.H.I.E.L.D. agent.

Falcon has high-tech wings.
He uses them to fly.

Ant-Man is a tech genius.

Ant-Man wears a special suit.
He uses it to shrink!

Wasp is a trained fighter.

Wasp has small wings.
She uses them to fly fast!

The universe is full of villains.

The Avengers battle
villains as a team!

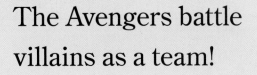

These are the Avengers.